THAT'S NOT FUNNY!

Jeanne Willis   Adrian Reynolds

ANDERSEN PRESS

For Harold Lazarus. Keep laughing. Lots of love, J.W.

For Otto Soloman Stone. A.R.

Other books by Jeanne Willis and Adrian Reynolds

WHO'S IN THE LOO?

Winner of the Red House Children's Book Award
and the Sheffield Children's Book Award

MINE'S BIGGER THAN YOURS!

First published in Great Britain in 2010 by Andersen Press Ltd.,
20 Vauxhall Bridge Road, London SW1V 2SA.
Published in Australia by Random House Australia Pty.,
Level 3, 100 Pacific Highway, North Sydney, NSW 2060.
Text copyright © Jeanne Willis, 2010.
Illustration copyright © Adrian Reynolds, 2010.
The rights of Jeanne Willis and Adrian Reynolds to be identified as
the author and illustrator of this work have been asserted by them
in accordance with the Copyright, Designs and Patents Act, 1988.
All rights reserved.
Colour separated in Switzerland by Photolitho AG, Zürich.
Printed and bound in Singapore by Tien Wah Press.

10   9   8   7   6   5   4   3   2   1

British Library Cataloguing in Publication Data available.

ISBN 978 1 84270 951 1

This book has been printed on acid-free paper

One day, just for a joke, Hyena put a banana skin on Giraffe's path.

Giraffe slipped on it and skidded straight into a tree –

KER-RANG!

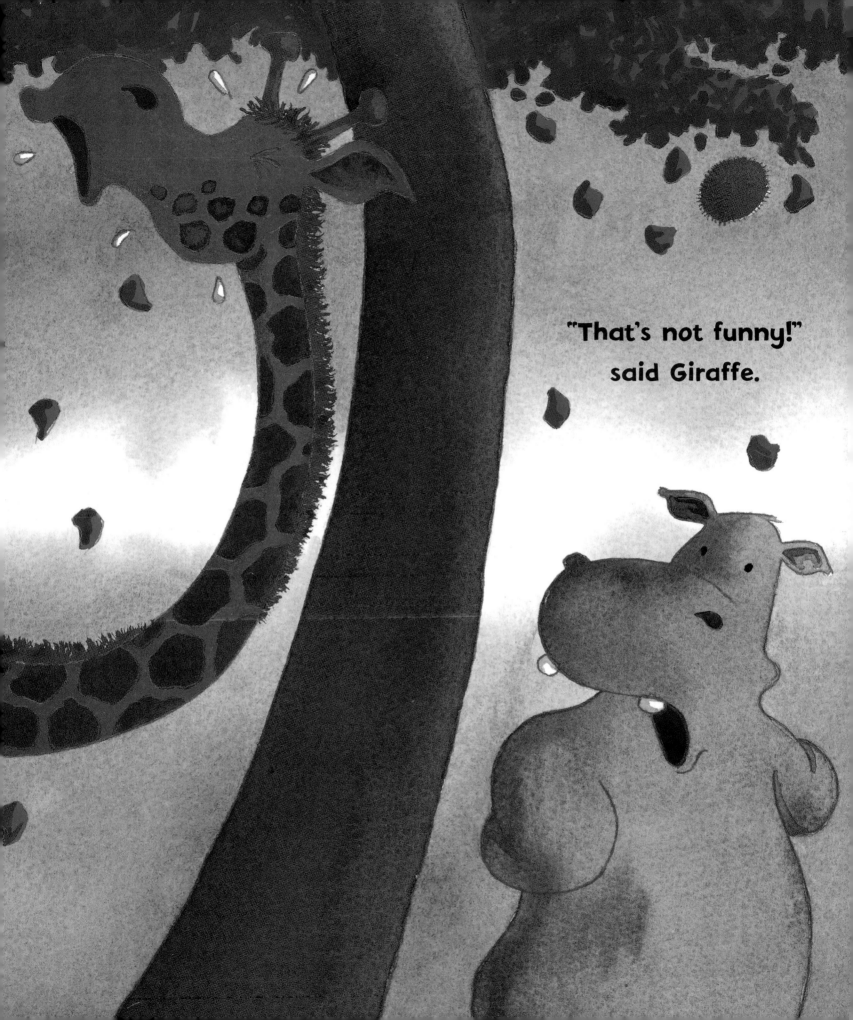

"That's not funny!"
said Giraffe.

But Hyena laughed and laughed, because when Giraffe skidded into the tree, a coconut fell and hit Hippo right on the head –

BINK!

"That's not funny!" said Hippo.

But Hyena laughed and laughed, because when
Hippo was hit on the head, he went so dizzy,
he stepped on Snake.

"That'sssssssssss not funny!" hissed Snake.

But Hyena laughed and laughed, because when Hippo stepped on Snake, Snake was so shocked, she bit Ostrich.

"That's not funny!" said Ostrich.

But Hyena laughed and laughed, because when Snake bit Ostrich, Ostrich was so sore she kicked Rhino and he fell into the swamp.

"That's not funny!" said Rhino.

But Hyena laughed and laughed, because when Rhino fell,
he catapulted Turtle right into the air . . .

Turtle torpedoed into Vulture . . .

. . . and Vulture
flopped
down
from
the
sky,
and landed on Zebra.

"That's not funny!" said Zebra.

But Hyena laughed and laughed, because Zebra tripped up Cheetah.

"That's not funny!" screeched Cheetah.

But Hyena laughed and laughed, because when Cheetah screeched, he startled Wildebeest.

"That's not funny!"
said Wildebeest.

But Hyena laughed and laughed, because Wildebeest
and all his startled friends were stampeding
towards Elephant, who'd gone to visit Giraffe.

Hyena couldn't wait to see what hilarious thing would happen to Elephant, so he hurried back to Giraffe's to get a good view.

But he was so keen not to miss the joke, he forgot about the banana skin he'd left on the path and he skidded into a tree - **KER-RANG!**

A coconut fell and hit him right on the head –

BINK!

He went so dizzy, he stepped right into . . .

a huge, steaming heap of

Elephant's

Poo!

"That's not funny!" said Hyena.

But oh, how all the other animals laughed and laughed and laughed and laughed and laughed . . .

and laughed and laughed and laughed.

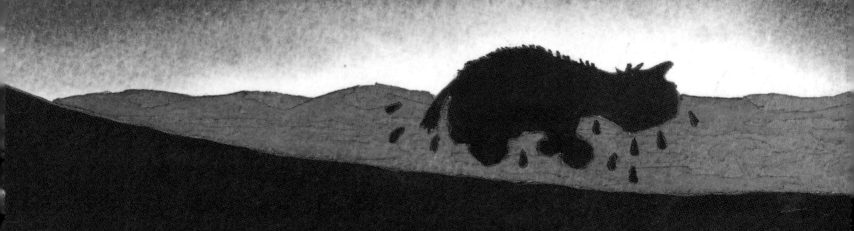